The Gingerbread Man

illustrated by Estelle Corke

Child's Play (International) Ltd
Ashworth Rd, Bridgemead, Swindon, SN5 7YD UK

Swindon   Auburn ME   Sydney

© 2007 Child's Play (International) Ltd   Printed in Heshan, China
ISBN 978-1-84643-078-7   L100312FUFT07120787

www.childs-play.com

10

Once upon a time, an old couple were baking gingerbread. They mixed flour and butter, molasses, sugar and eggs, and cut some of the mixture into the shape of a little man. They popped currants where his eyes and nose should be, and made a cheeky smile out of sugar icing.

Then the old lady put
him in the oven to bake.

"That smells delicious," said the old man
to his wife, a little later.
"Yes," she agreed. "I can't wait to taste it!"

All of a sudden, there was a tiny banging noise
from the oven. "What's that?" asked the old man.
Before they could even open the oven door,
out burst the gingerbread man.

"Ouch!" he shouted. "It's much too hot in there!"
"Wait!" called the old woman.
"We're going to eat you later!"
"No way!" he laughed. "Run, run, as fast as you can!
You can't catch me, I'm the gingerbread man!"
And he leapt straight through the window.

In the yard, a chicken was pecking in the dirt,
when the gingerbread man landed in front of her.
"Come here, little man!" clucked the chicken.
"I love gingerbread!"

The old man and woman
came rushing out of the kitchen.
"Stop that gingerbread man!" they shouted.
"I don't think so!" replied the gingerbread man.
"Run, run, as fast as you can! You can't catch me,
I'm the gingerbread man!"
And he vaulted straight over the fence.

As the gingerbread man came dashing along the path, closely followed by the old lady, the old man and the chicken, he was spotted by a dog out for a walk.

"Wait for me!" barked the dog.
"I love the smell of gingerbread!"

"No chance!" called back the gingerbread man.
"You won't get close! Run, run, as fast as you can!
You can't catch me, I'm the gingerbread man!"
And he disappeared into the bushes.

The gingerbread man ran as fast
as lightning through the bushes,
closely followed by the old lady,
the old man, the chicken and the dog,
and into a meadow where a cow was grazing.

"You look lovely," she drooled. "Come a little closer!"
"Not a chance!" called the gingerbread man.

"You're much too slow! Run, run, as fast as you can!
You can't catch me, I'm the gingerbread man!"

A horse was grazing in the next field,
when the gingerbread man came rushing by,
closely followed by the old lady, the old man,
the chicken, the dog and the cow.

"Great!" neighed the horse. "I love chases!"
"You're joking!" jeered the gingerbread man.
"You'll never catch me! Run, run, as fast as you can!
You can't catch me, I'm the gingerbread man!"

The gingerbread man
ran and ran. He ran across
meadows and fields.
He jumped fences,
bushes and streams.

He even had time
to sit on a branch
and tease everyone
and everything chasing him.
"Slowcoaches!" he shouted.
"Run, run, as fast as you can!
You can't catch me,
I'm the gingerbread man!"

The gingerbread man came to a river.
"Oh no!" he groaned. "I can't swim! I'll get all soggy!"
Just at that moment, a fox came along.

"Hello," said the fox. "Are you lost?"
"No," said the gingerbread man,
"but I do need to cross the river quite quickly."

The fox looked at the chasing figures in the distance.
"I am a good swimmer," he suggested.
"Just jump on my tail, and I will take you across."
So the gingerbread man jumped onto the fox's tail,
and they waded
into the river.

As they reached the middle
of the river, the gingerbread man
felt his toes getting damp and spongy.
"Mr Fox!" he yelled. "My feet are getting wet!"
"Don't worry," replied the fox, with a clever grin.
"Jump on my back, and you will keep perfectly dry."
The gingerbread man did as he was told,
but soon his knees began to crumble in the wet.

The fox grinned even more.
"The driest place I have," he said,
"is right here, on the tip of my nose. Hurry!"
So the gingerbread man jumped as far
as he could, right onto the fox's nose.
He turned to look at the crowd
gathered on the riverbank.
"I'm the gingerbread man!" he yelled out.
"You won't ever catch me!"
"But I will!" snapped the fox.

And he tipped
the gingerbread man
straight off his nose and
into his gaping mouth!

Everyone turned for home,
hungry after all the running they had done.
"Never mind," said the old man.
"We've still got some
gingerbread mixture left."

"Thank goodness," said the old woman.
"But let's make something slower this time.
How about a gingerbread snail?"